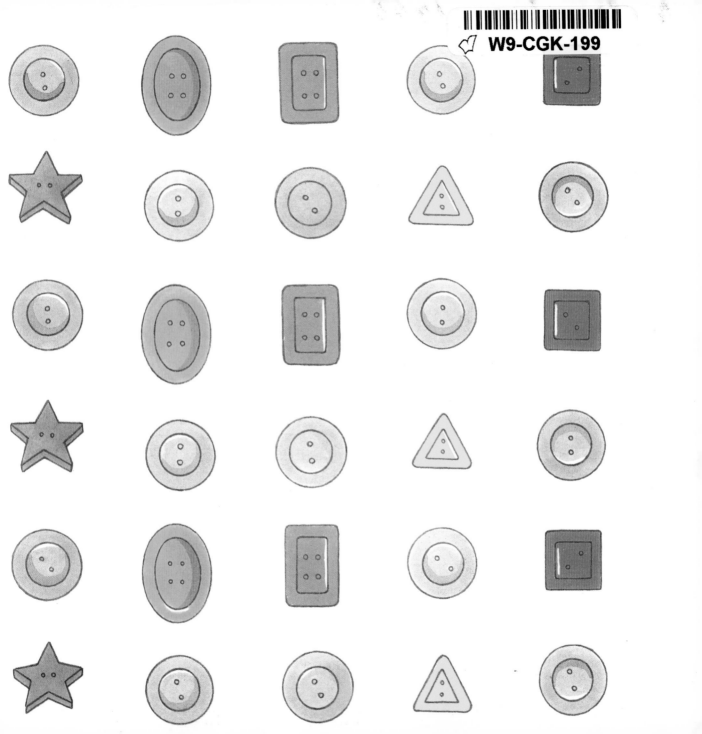

A DERRYDALE
BOOK

BIG BEAR
AND THE BLUE BUTTON

Written by Stephanie Laslett

Illustrated by John Blackman

Derrydale Books
New York • Avenel

Wake up Big Bear!
Wake up Morris Mouse!

Morris
Mouse

Time to get up.

Time to
do our
exercises.

Stretch
up high.

Morris
Mouse

Bend down low.

What has Big
Bear found?
Is this your
round blue
button?

No. My buttons are **red** and shaped like **squares**.

Hello, Percy Pig. Is this your **round blue** button?
No. My buttons are **yellow** and shaped like **triangles**.

Boris Badger has arrived.
Is this your round **blue button**?
No. My buttons
are **green** and
shaped like
rectangles.

There's Olive Owl walking past.

Is this your **round blue** button Olive?

No. My buttons are **pink** and shaped like **ovals**.

Has this **round blue** button popped off your bag?

No. My bag has buttons which
are **purple** and shaped like **stars**.

Whose is this **round blue** button?

Hoo, hoo, hoo! hoots Olive Owl. Your trousers have **round blue** buttons.

It is *your* button Big Bear!

It popped off when you bent
down to touch your toes!

Now we all have our buttons!

Blue Round

Red Square

Yellow Triangle

Green Rectangle

Pink Oval

Purple Star